My meow is **LOUD**.

Mine is soft.

I am **TALL**.

And I am short.

I am **chubby**.

And I am skinny.

My tail is **long**.

Mine is **stubby**.

I am *shy*.

And I am **not**.

We're all different but
we're all kitty cats.

Published by dreamBIG Press
Washington, DC
www.dreambigpress.com

Distributed by Emerald Book Company

For ordering information or special discounts for bulk purchases, please contact Emerald Book Company at PO Box 91869, Austin, TX 78709, 512.891.6100.

Design and composition by Scott Woldin
Cover design by Gut Instinct Creative LLC
Illustrations by Nicolás Milano

Publisher's Cataloging-In-Publication Data
(Prepared by The Donohue Group, Inc.)
Goodman, Peter J.
  We're all different but we're all kitty cats. First day of school / by Peter J. Goodman ; illustrated by Nicolás Milano.
    p. : col. ill. ; cm.
  Summary: When Carlos announces on the first day of school that he is a hairless kitty cat, his feline schoolmates show the way to respect his differences and help him discover what makes him unique.
    Interest age group: 004-006.
    ISBN: 978-0-9850683-0-1

    1. Individual differences--Juvenile fiction. 2. Cats--Juvenile fiction. 3. Bullying--Prevention--Juvenile fiction.
4. Individuality--Fiction. 5. Cats--Fiction. 6. Bullying--Fiction. I. Milano, Nicolás. II. Title. III. Title: First day of school
PZ7.G66 Wer 2012
[E]   2012934036

Part of the Tree Neutral® program, which offsets the number of trees consumed in the production and printing of this book by taking proactive steps, such as planting trees in direct proportion to the number of trees used: www.treeneutral.com

TreeNeutral®

Manufactured by iPrinting on acid-free paper
Manufactured in Shanghai, China in May, 2012
Batch No. 1

12 13 14 15 16 17   10 9 8 7 6 5 4 3 2 1

First Edition

For Dylan, Gavin, Maris,
Ethan, Dylan & María

WE'RE ALL DIFFERENT BUT WE'RE ALL KITTY CATS

First Day of School

By Peter J. Goodman

Illustrated by Nicolás Milano

dreamBIG press

"Carlos, wake up sweetie.

It's time to get ready for school,"
his mommy said.

"Are you excited for your first day of school?" asked his mommy.

"I'm nervous," Carlos said.

"It's okay to be nervous.
You're going to make some very
nice new friends," said his mommy.

As Carlos walked to school at Meowville Elementary, he saw all the kitty cats running to get to class on time.

"I'll go first.
My name is Miss Bobsie and
I wear funky glasses.
My favorite color is green."

"Who would
like to go next?"

"ME!
I'm Dylan!"

"I have a bushy tail and I like to play tennis."

"I'm Sammy and this is my friend Mort the mouse. I love to tell jokes."

Sammy asked the class, "What kind of cake do mice eat?" No one answered.

"Cheese-cake!" Everyone laughed.

"I'm Marla.

"I have blue eyes and I like to ride my scooter."

"My name is Flo and I have white fur."

"I like to play dress up with my best friend Marla."

"I'm Vinny. I have six brothers and two sisters."

"Vinny, can you tell the class
one more thing about yourself?"
asked Miss Bobsie.

"Yeah.
I like football," said Vinny.

And then Carlos stood up.

"My name is Carlos and I like to read books."

"Carlos, can you please share with the class one more thing about yourself?" asked Miss Bobsie.

"I have no fur," said Carlos.

The whole class laughed.

"Quiet down class," said Miss Bobsie.

Carlos sat down and all the kitty cats stared at him.

He put his head down on his desk and began to cry.

After school, as Flo and Marla walked home, they talked about what happened to Carlos in class.

"I feel bad that everyone laughed at Carlos," said Flo.

"Me too. We didn't mean to make him cry," Marla said.

Just as Marla and Flo approached the gate to leave school they saw Vinny and Carlos.

Marla and Flo walked up to Vinny and Carlos.
"Vinny, leave Carlos alone," Flo said.

"Carlos and I were just talking,"
Vinny said, as Carlos looked down
at the ground.

"Talking, Vinny? I don't think so.
You're hurting Carlos' feelings.
Find a kitty cat your own size," said Marla.

Vinny stared at Marla and Flo and then he walked away.

"Carlos, are you okay?"
asked Flo.

"Yeah, I'm okay...I guess."

Marla and Flo walked
with Carlos all the way home.

Carlos went straight to his room and sat on his bed with his paws over his eyes.

His mommy heard him crying.

She knocked on the door and slowly opened it.

"What's wrong, honey?" his mommy asked.

"No one likes me at school," said Carlos.

"What do you mean, honey?" his mommy asked.

"Everyone laughed at me today."

"Why did they laugh at you?" asked his mommy.

"Because I don't have any fur."
"Vinny even said I was not a kitty cat," Carlos said.

"Even if you don't have fur,
you're still a kitty cat," said his mommy.
"I don't feel like a kitty cat. Everyone else has fur but I don't," Carlos said.

"Carlos, you are a very handsome kitty cat.
Let's look in the mirror together," said his mommy.

"I already know what
I look like, mommy," Carlos said.

"Well you're not looking close enough.
Let me show you what I see."

"Now give me a smile and look
into the mirror, Carlos," his mommy said.

"Look at your eyes. They're as blue as the sea.
Look at your smile. It's as bright as the sun.
Look at your ears. They point straight to the sky."

"But I still don't have any fur," said Carlos.

"Well, each kitty in your class looks different, right? But they are still kitty cats," his mommy said.

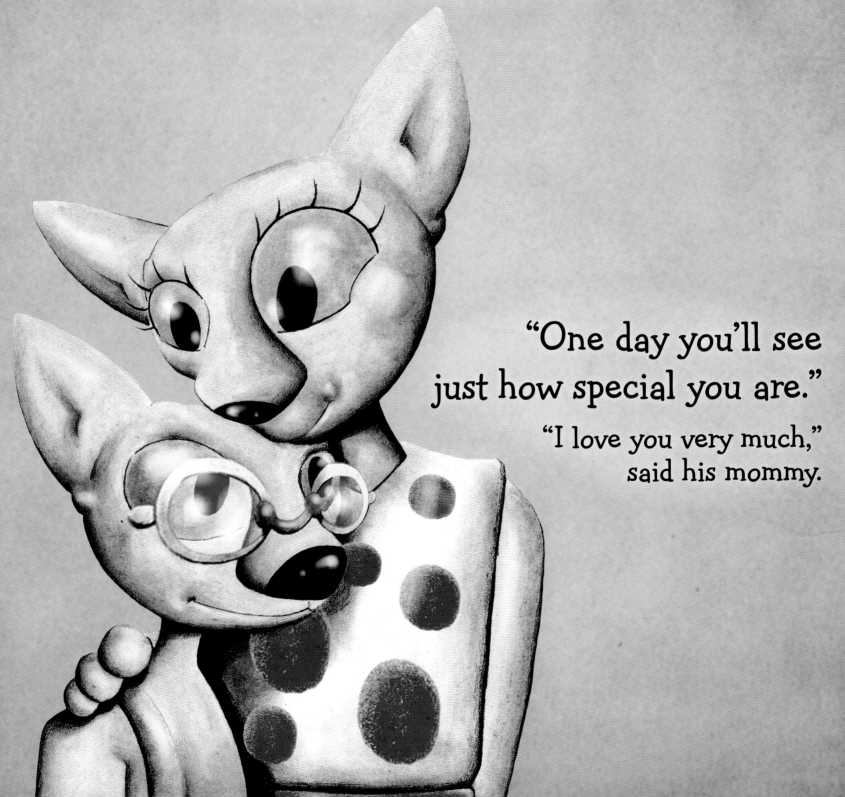

"One day you'll see just how special you are."

"I love you very much," said his mommy.

The next morning,
Carlos went to school.

He was scared to see Vinny and the
kitty cats who laughed at him the day before.

When Carlos walked into the classroom,
he sat all the way in the back.

Miss Bobsie stood in front of the chalkboard. "We're going to learn our A, B, C's today," she said.

"Who knows what letter this is?" Miss Bobsie asked.

Three paws went
up in the air.

She pointed to Sammy.

"It's an A," Sammy said.

Then Miss Bobsie wrote another letter on the chalkboard.
Two paws went up in the air.

Miss Bobsie pointed to Allie.

"It's a B," Allie said.

Miss Bobsie wrote another letter on the chalkboard.

"Class, who knows what letter comes next?"

Only one paw went up.

Miss Bobsie pointed to Dylan.

"It's C.
C comes next,"
said Dylan.

"Okay class, what is the next letter?" asked Miss Bobsie.

Everyone was silent.

Miss Bobsie asked Vinny, "Do you know what comes after C?"

"I don't know," Vinny said.

"Can anyone help Vinny out?" Miss Bobsie asked.

Way in the back of the classroom,
a tiny paw rose in the air.

"Carlos, can you share with the class what letter comes after C?"
He looked around at all of the other kitty cats before he spoke.

"Let's see...A...B...C..."

"D...E-F-G-H-I-J-K-L-M-N-O-P-Q-R-S-T-U-V-W-X-Y and Z!"

Miss Bobsie and all of the kitty cats were shocked that Carlos knew the entire alphabet!

All of a sudden, Sammy started to clap and then all the kitty cats joined in. Even Vinny.

Carlos smiled and thought,
"My mommy is right,
I am special and I am a kitty cat."

have fun while communicating with your kids.
you may be surprised what your child says!

At dreamBIG, we know the more you communicate with your child, the better your relationship will be.

Below are some questions for you to use to start a conversation with your child. Because your child is processing the story in his or her own way, there are no right or wrong answers. Of course, you'll guide your child in the right direction in terms of bullying behavior and feelings. But remember, have fun!

- If you were asked to share two things about yourself with your class, what would you say?
- Who was your favorite kitty cat? Why?
- Why did the kitty cats laugh at Carlos?
- How do you think Carlos felt?
- Why do you think Vinny picked on Carlos after school?
- What did Flo do after school that helped Carlos?
- What did Carlos do when he went home?
- Did his Mom make him feel better?
- What does your family do to make you feel better?
- What makes you feel special at school? At home?
- Who else could Carlos have talked to about being picked on?
- Is there anything you can do if you see someone being picked on?

fun facts about kitty cats

- A cat will almost never "meow" at another cat. Cats use this sound for humans.

- Cats don't think of themselves as small humans. Rather, they think of us as large cats!

- Cats are the most popular pet in the world!

- A cat can be either right-pawed or left-pawed.

- The more cats are spoken to, the more they will speak to you.

- Kittens begin dreaming when they are just one week old.

dreamBIG has lots of fun activities and educational resources for kids and parents on our website at **www.dreambigpress.com**.

about dreamBIG

At dreamBIG, we view kids' books as a way to bring adults and kids together. They provide excellent opportunities for parents to talk and communicate with their children about important social issues—early in their development. And, books are sure to stir your child's imagination!

We hope that our books will start conversations that last a lifetime.
We dream BIG.

not just a another kids' book series...

The *We're All Different But We're All Kitty Cat* book series tackles important topics that relate to developing social and emotional skills. With vivid illustrations and compelling narratives, each book ends with questions that help parents engage and communicate with their child.

topics to be covered in the series

- Being different
- Bullying
- Communication
- Confidence
- Empathy
- Illness & loss
- Independence
- Making & losing friends
- Managing emotions
- Scared of the dark

peter j. goodman

Peter spent much of his childhood dreaming big. Whenever he spoke, he had some kind of tale to tell and always relayed his stories with great enthusiasm, which he brings to his writing today. A multimedia children's book author, Peter's Kitty Cat series brings adults and kids together to discuss important social issues from early childhood. The series encourages discussion and dialogue through thought-provoking and edge-of-your-seat narratives. Peter's first book, *Win-Win Career Negotiations* was published by Penguin Books in 2002, and he has been featured in the *Wall Street Journal*, *The Washington Post*, *Chicago Tribune* and *Publishers Weekly*. He currently resides in Washington, DC.

creative development

Nicolás Milano, Illustrator
Scott Woldin, Design & Layout

child development & education

JoAnn B. Sanders, Ph.D., M.Ed.

Stay tuned for our next Kitty Cat book!
www.dreambigpress.com

No kitty cats were harmed or feelings hurt while making this book.